S0-BUA-284

EVERYTHING IS GRAPE!

WRITTEN BY
ALASTAIR HEIM

ILLUSTRATED BY
MICHELLE TRAN

HENRY HOLT AND COMPANY • NEW YORK

CORNER MARKET

BELL ST.

PARKL

OPEN

FOR TIM TIMMERMAN . . .
WHO IS ONE GRAPE FRIEND
—A. H.

FOR GREY
—M. T.

HENRY HOLT AND COMPANY, PUBLISHERS SINCE 1866
HENRY HOLT® IS A REGISTERED TRADEMARK OF MACMILLAN PUBLISHING GROUP, LLC.
120 BROADWAY, NEW YORK, NY 10271 • MACKIDS.COM

TEXT COPYRIGHT © 2024 BY ALASTAIR HEIM.
ILLUSTRATIONS COPYRIGHT © 2024 BY MICHELLE TRAN. ALL RIGHTS RESERVED.

OUR BOOKS MAY BE PURCHASED IN BULK FOR PROMOTIONAL, EDUCATIONAL, OR
BUSINESS USE. PLEASE CONTACT YOUR LOCAL BOOKSELLER OR THE MACMILLAN
CORPORATE AND PREMIUM SALES DEPARTMENT AT (800) 221-7945 EXT. 5442
OR BY EMAIL AT MACMILLANSPECIALMARKETS@MACMILLAN.COM.

LIBRARY OF CONGRESS CONTROL NUMBER: 2023948824

FIRST EDITION, 2024
BOOK DESIGN BY MINA CHUNG
THE ART FOR THIS BOOK WAS CREATED DIGITALLY.
PRINTED IN CHINA BY RR DONNELLEY ASIA PRINTING SOLUTIONS LTD.,
DONGGUAN CITY, GUANGDONG PROVINCE

ISBN 978-1-250-89141-9
10 9 8 7 6 5 4 3 2 1

MEADOWS
PARK

YOU COULD SAY IT IS AN ODD-SHAPED, BOX-SHAPED GRAPE.

NO. YOU COULD *NOT* SAY THAT,

BECAUSE IT IS A BOX.